THE LITTLE RABBIT WHO WANTED RED WINGS

The Little Rabbit Who Wanted Red Wings

by CAROLYN SHERWIN BAILEY

Illustrated by DOROTHY GRIDER

PLATT & MUNK, *Publishers*
NEW YORK

Once upon a time there was a little White Rabbit with two beautiful pink ears and two bright red eyes and four soft little feet — SUCH a pretty little white rabbit, but he wasn't happy.

Just think, this little White Rabbit wanted to be somebody else
instead of the nice little rabbit that
he was.

When Mr. Bushy Tail, the gray

squirrel, went by, the little White
Rabbit would say to his Mummy:
"Oh, Mummy, I WISH I had a
long gray tail like Mr. Bushy
Tail's."

And when Mr. Porcupine went
by, the little White Rabbit would
say to his Mummy:
"Oh, Mummy, I WISH I had a

back full of bristles like Mr. Porcu-pine's."

And when Miss Puddle-Duck went by in her two little red rub-

bers, the little White Rabbit would
say:

"Oh, Mummy, I WISH I had a
pair of red rubbers like Miss Puddle-Duck's."

So he went on wishing and wishing until his Mummy was quite
tired out with his wishing. One
day Old Mr. Ground Hog heard
him wishing.

Old Mr. Ground Hog is very wise indeed, so he said to the little White Rabbit:

"Why don't you go down to Wishing Pond, and if you look in

the water at yourself and turn
around three times in a circle, you
will get your wish."

So the little White Rabbit
trotted off, all alone by himself

through the woods, until he **came**
to a little pool of green water lying
in a low tree stump, and that was
the Wishing Pond. There was a
little, LITTLE bird, all red, sitting

on the edge of the Wishing Pond to
get a drink, and as soon as the little
White Rabbit saw him he began to
wish again:

"Oh, I wish I had a pair of little

red wings!" he said. Just then he looked in the Wishing Pond and he saw his little white face. Then he turned around three times and something happened. He began to have a queer feeling in his shoul-

ders, like he felt in his mouth when he was cutting teeth. It was his wings coming through. So he sat all day in the woods by the Wishing Pond waiting for them to grow, and, by and by, when it was

almost sundown, he started home
to see his Mummy and show her,
because he had a beautiful pair of
long, trailing red wings.

But by the time he reached home
it was getting dark, and when he

went to the hole at the foot of
a big tree where he lived, his
Mummy didn't know him. No, she
really and truly did not know him,
because, you see, she had never
seen a rabbit with red wings in all

her life. And so the little White
Rabbit had to go out again, because his Mummy wouldn't let
him get into his own bed. He had
to go out and look for some place
to sleep all night.

He went and went until he came
to Mr. Bushy Tail's house, and he
rapped on the door and said:

"Please, kind Mr. Bushy Tail,
may I sleep in your house all
night?"

But Mr. Bushy Tail opened his door a crack and then he slammed it tight shut again. You see he had never seen a rabbit with red wings in all his life.

So the little White Rabbit went
on and on until he came to Miss
Puddle-Duck's nest down by the
marsh and he said:

"Please, kind Miss Puddle-Duck,

may I sleep in your nest all night?"
But Miss Puddle-Duck poked her
head up out of her nest just a little
way and then she shut her eyes
and stretched her wings out so far
that she covered her whole nest,
and said, "no, no, no, go away."

You see she had never seen a
rabbit with red wings in all her life.

So the little White Rabbit went
on and on until he came to Old Mr.
Ground Hog's hole and Old Mr.
Ground Hog let him sleep with
him all night, but the hole had

beechnuts spread all over it. Old
Mr. Ground Hog liked to sleep on
them, but they hurt the little White
Rabbit and made him very uncom-
fortable before morning.

When morning came, the little
White Rabbit decided to try his
wings and fly a little, so he climbed
up on a hill and spread his wings
and sailed off, but he landed in a

low bush all full of prickles, and his
four feet got mixed up with twigs
so he couldn't get down.

"Mummy, Mummy, Mummy,
come and help me!" he called.

His Mummy didn't hear him, but
Old Mr. Ground Hog did, and he

came and helped the little White
Rabbit out of the prickly bush.

"Don't you want your red
wings?" Mr. Ground Hog asked.

"No, NO!" said the little White
Rabbit.

"Well," said the Old Ground

Hog, "why don't you go down to
the Wishing Pond and wish them
off again?"

So the little White Rabbit went

down to the Wishing Pond and he saw his face in it. Then he turned around three times, and, sure enough, his red wings were gone.

Then he went home to his Mummy, who knew him right away and was so glad to see him; and the little White Rabbit never, NEVER again wished to be something different from what he really was.